The Sparkle Box

Written by JILL HARDIE ✎ Illustrated by CHRISTINE KORNACKI

ideals children's books.
Nashville, Tennessee

ISBN-13: 978-0-8249-5647-9

Published by Ideals Children's Books
An imprint of Ideals Publications
A Guideposts Company
Nashville, Tennessee
www.idealsbooks.com

Design by Georgina Chidlow-Rucker

Color separations by Precision Color Graphics, Franklin, Wisconsin
Printed and bound in China

Leo_ Jul13 _ 5

Library of Congress Cataloging-in-Publication Data

Hardie, Jill, date.
  The Sparkle Box : a gift with the power to change Christmas / written
by Jill Hardie ; illustrated by Christine Kornacki.
    p. cm.
  ISBN-13: 978-0-8249-5647-9 (hardcover : alk. paper)
[1. Christmas—Fiction. 2. Charity—Fiction. 3. Gifts—Fiction. 4.
Conduct of life—Fiction. 5. Christian life—Fiction.] I. Kornacki,
Christine, ill. II. Title.
  PZ7.H2176Sp 2012
  [E]—dc23

                        2012006590

To Tim, Katie, Jack, Mom, Steve, and Marykay
With all my love—J.H.

For my parents, my perpetual inspiration
—C.K.

Dear reader, you are the light of the world.

Make it sparkle.

Snowflakes swirled through the air as Sam and his mom stopped to look in the toy store window. With Christmas only a few weeks away, Sam needed to make his Christmas list. He tugged on his mom's sleeve and pointed to the train. He loved the shiny red engine.

Later, as Sam and his mom curled up on the couch to read a Christmas book, something sparkly on the mantel caught his eye. "Mom, is that a present for me?" he asked.

Sam's mom tousled his hair. "It's a special gift, called a Sparkle Box. We'll open it together later, but we need to fill it first."

Sam was excited—but it was hard to wait!

Driving home from school the next day, Sam's mom stopped at a building he had never been to before. She asked him to help her carry in some food and blankets.

Sam peeked into the bag he was carrying and noticed a box of macaroni and cheese—his favorite! "What are we doing with this stuff, Mom?"

She smiled and said, "We're giving it to people who don't have enough food to eat or blankets to keep them warm."

But inside the building, Sam didn't see
anyone who looked cold or hungry—just a
nice lady with a big smile who thanked them.

On the way home, they drove by the park. It was dusk, and the pretty Christmas lights had just come on. As they stopped at a traffic light, Sam noticed someone on a bench, curled up and sleeping.

His mother noticed too. "That's someone who may get one of our blankets," she said softly. "He doesn't have anywhere to live."

Sam felt bad. It would be sad not to have a home to live in.

Peace

Faith

Hope

Sam hung up his coat. It was good to be home. As he sat at the kitchen table to have a snack, he noticed the Sparkle Box gleaming on the mantel.

"Mom, did you put anything in the Sparkle Box yet?" he asked shyly.

"Well, actually, I did put something in it today," she answered. "But it's still not ready to be opened. We need to add a couple more things to it."

Sam wondered what was inside.

The days flew by and soon it was time for one of Sam's favorite events, the Christmas party at his dad's office. There was always lots of delicious food and a present for every child at the party!

Sam's dad thanked everyone for coming. He talked about how blessed they were, when many people in the world struggle for something as simple as clean water to drink. He said a village in Africa would receive a special gift this year, thanks to money donated by employees and their families. The gift was a well that would provide clean water for the entire village!

Sam asked his mom if his family helped. "Yes, dear, we did." He looked around. The grownups were smiling, but he saw tears too. "Happy tears," his mom whispered.

As his dad tucked him into bed that night, Sam thought about his Christmas list, and that reminded him of another present.

"Daddy, did you and Mom fill up the Sparkle Box yet?" Sam asked.

"Well, we added something to it tonight, but it's still not ready to be opened."

Sam drifted off to sleep, imagining what could be inside.

A few days later, Sam was filled with excitement as he shopped with his mom. Tomorrow was his school party! There was a Christmas tree called a mitten tree, where the kids could hang mittens, hats, and scarves for people who needed them.

Sam picked out the biggest pair of mittens he could find.

He also bought a candy bar for himself, with his own money.

When he turned to leave, Sam heard the tinkling of bells. He looked up and saw the man from the park bench coming in the door. The man seemed tired. Sam looked at the candy bar in his hand and thought about the mittens in his bag. He looked at the man's hands. They looked cold. Sam's heart began to pound.

As quick as a wink, Sam slipped his candy bar into the bag with the mittens and pressed the bag into the man's hands. Sam ran out the door, shouting, "Merry Christmas!"

His mom gave him a hug. "I'm proud of you," she whispered. "I know that wasn't easy, but you brought a little light into his world tonight."

Sam asked his mom if they could drive by the park. As he watched the flame on a giant candle blink on and off, he thought about how unfair it was that some people didn't have a home to live in or food to eat.

Soon it was Christmas Eve—the most special night of the year! Sam and his family gathered at their church for a Christmas Eve service.

They sang songs and listened to the story of the first Christmas.

Then, in the darkened sanctuary, a single candle was lit. That candle was used to light other candles, and soon everyone was carefully passing the flame from one person to the next, until the whole room was filled with a magical light. Sam looked around. How lovely, how peaceful they all looked as they shared the light!

On Christmas morning,
Sam ran downstairs as fast as he
could. Under the tree was the train
with the shiny red engine! And what was
that? The Sparkle Box! Sam could hardly
wait to open it.

He sat on his mom's lap with his dad snuggled in close. Sam slowly lifted the lid of the box. Inside, there were just a few pieces of paper with words written on them. Puzzled, he took the papers out and began to read the words out loud.

Mittens and a candy bar given to someone in need

Warm blankets and food for the homeless

A well in Africa that will provide clean drinking water

Sam's mom explained, "Sam, the Sparkle Box is our gift to Jesus on Christmas Day, His birthday."

He was confused. "But we didn't give Jesus a gift. We gave things to people who needed them."

His mom smiled. "You're right, and no gift could make Jesus happier. He taught us that whatever we do for people in need, we do for Him. So each year we'll think of some special gifts to give Jesus. We'll write down these gifts and put them in the Sparkle Box. On Christmas morning, we'll open the box and read out loud the gifts we gave in honor of His birthday."

Sam thought about the man curled up on the park bench. The mittens and the soft blankets. The well that would bring clean water to a village in Africa.

He looked at his mom and smiled through tears. "Happy tears," Sam whispered.

Will you put a Sparkle Box under your Christmas tree?

What will you put inside? Warm blankets for the homeless? Food for the hungry? Maybe you'll sponsor a child's education or give funds for life-saving medical care. Be creative and think of things that will make Jesus happy!

Expand the enclosed box and fold in the flaps, closing both ends, to assemble your own Sparkle Box! Or have fun making a homemade Sparkle Box by decorating a shoebox with paint, glitter, wrapping paper, or stickers!

Place your Sparkle Box under your Christmas tree. Throughout the Christmas season, write down the special gifts you're giving in honor of Jesus' birthday, and put them in your Sparkle Box. On Christmas morning, open the Sparkle Box and read your gifts out loud. Bask in the warm glow of light that comes from giving a gift to the greatest gift of all: Jesus Christ.

"You are the light of the world—like a city on a mountain, glowing in the night for all to see."
—Matthew 5:14 (NLT)

"The King will reply, 'Truly I tell you, whatever you did for one of the least of these brothers and sisters of mine, you did for me.'"
—Matthew 25:40 (NIV)

Visit the author's website at www.TheSparkleBox.com for more information and ideas, or to share your Sparkle Box story.